The Dead Sea Squirrels Series

Squirreled Away

Boy Meets Squirrels

Nutty Study Buddies

Squirrelnapped!

Tree-mendous Trouble

Whirly Squirrelies

Merle of Nazareth

A Dusty Donkey Detour

Jingle Squirrels

Squirreled Away

Mike Nawrocki

Illustrated by Luke Séguin-Magee

Tyndale House Publishers
Carol Stream, Illinois

Visit Tyndale's website for kids at tyndale.com/kids.

Visit the author's website at mikenawrocki.com.

Designed by Libby Dykstra

Edited by Sarah Rubio

Published in association with the literary agency of Brentwood Studios, 1550 McEwen, Suite 300 PNB 17, Franklin, TN 37067.

For manufacturing information regarding this product, please call 1-800-323-9400.

For information about special discounts for bulk purchases, please contact Tyndale House Publishers at csresponse@tyndale.com, or call 1-800-323-9400.

Library of Congress Cataloging-in-Publication Data
Names: Nawrocki, Michael, author.
Title: Squirreled away / Mike Nawrocki.
Description: Carol Stream, Illinois : Tyndale House Publishers, Inc., [2019] | Series: Dead sea squirrels | Summary: Ten-year-old Michael sneaks into a cave near the Dead Sea where his father has been working and finds a pair of 2,000-year-old squirrels, which he stows in his backpack and takes home to Tennessee.
Identifiers: LCCN 2018037427 | ISBN 9781496434982 (sc)
Subjects: | CYAC: Squirrels--Fiction. | Christian life—Fiction. | Dead Sea (Israel and Jordan)—Fiction.
Classification: LCC PZ7.N185 Sq 2019 | DDC [Fic]—dc23 LC record available at https://lccn.loc.gov/2018037427

Printed in the United States of America

27 26 25 24 23 22 21
10 9 8 7 6 5 4

To Michael—

Though you are now an adult, you will always be my little boy. I hope your childhood was as adventurous and enjoyable for you as it was for me.

With love and pride, Dad

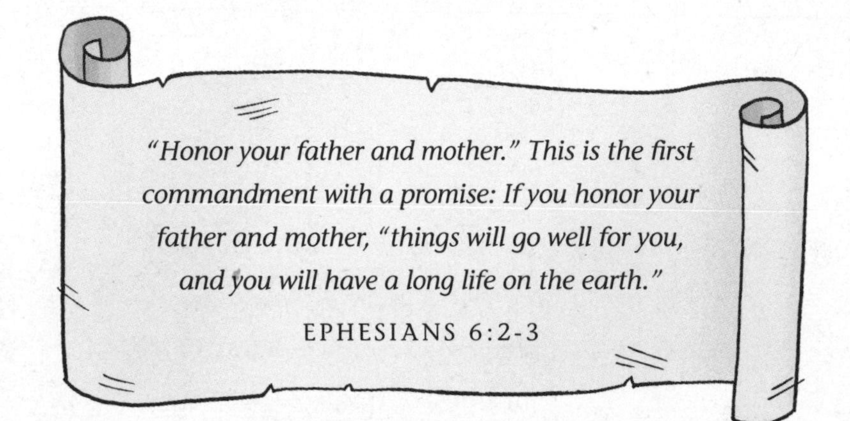

"Honor your father and mother." This is the first commandment with a promise: If you honor your father and mother, "things will go well for you, and you will have a long life on the earth."

EPHESIANS 6:2-3

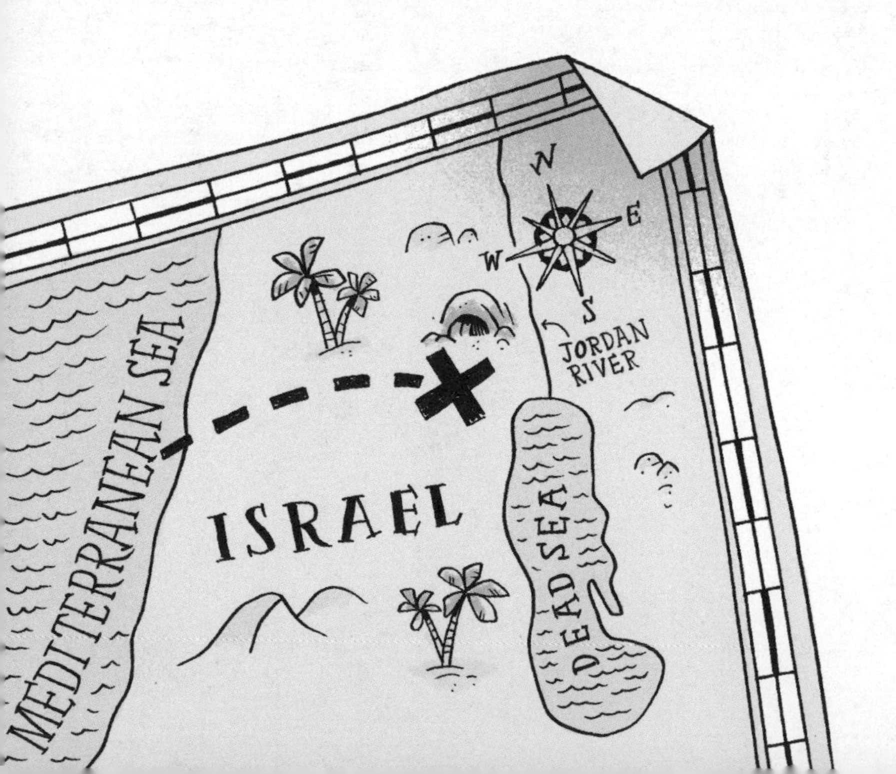

CHAPTER 1

ISRAEL, NEAR THE DEAD SEA
PRESENT DAY

Michael and Justin had been best friends ever since kindergarten, and when our story begins, they were a few days away from being fifth graders at Walnut Creek Elementary School. On this exact day, however, they were exploring a cave in the Middle East. If you're wondering where the Middle East is, look for *east* on a map and go to the middle. If you can't find east, just take a right at the Mediterranean Sea.

And if you're curious about *why* Michael and Justin were there . . . we'll get to that later.

"What is *that*?" Michael questioned, pointing his flashlight at something on a small ledge popping out from the rock wall a few feet above Justin's head. "You think it's some kind of animal?"

"Whatever it is, it's not moving," Justin replied.

"Maybe it's a bat," Michael suggested.

"Bats hang upside down," Justin said.

"Maybe it's a dead bat? That would be cool." Michael grinned.

Justin grimaced. "That would be disgusting."

"You *do* know a pet bat would make us the coolest kids in the fifth grade, right?" Michael said.

"A *dead* pet bat?" Justin raised his eyebrows.

As the two friends debated the value of a dead bat, the alarm on Justin's wristwatch went off.

"Oh no!" Justin said, looking

down at the rubbery band around his wrist. "We have to go!"

Michael stood on his tiptoes. "Give me a quick boost so I can see what's up there."

"We don't have time! If we're late for dinner again, your dad will kill us!"

"Relax. We're not going to be late," Michael assured his friend. "Just give me a boost."

Justin knew Michael well enough to realize that arguing with him would only waste more time, so he reluctantly assumed the boosting position. Michael placed his right shoe in Justin's cupped hands then stepped up and wedged his left shoe into a small crack in the cave wall. As Michael pushed himself up with his left leg toward the mystery ledge, his foot slipped out of the crack, and he fell face first into the wall. Justin held helplessly onto Michael's right foot as Michael's face slid down the gravelly wall and onto the dusty cave floor.

"Owwwwww," Michael groaned, his voice muffled by the dirt.

A second alarm sounded on Justin's watch. "Time's up. Let's go!"

CHAPTER 2

Nothing bothered Justin more than being late. If he wasn't at least 30 minutes early to school, he started to sweat. Inside of 15 minutes, he broke out into hives. The one time he was five minutes tardy, he nearly exploded. Running toward the cave entrance in danger of being late for dinner the second night in a row, Justin was in complete panic mode. That's probably why he ran straight past the turn he should have made.

Michael, jogging carelessly behind his friend and digging cave pebbles out of his nose, assumed Justin knew where he was going.

After a number of minutes of running past unrecognizable cave features, the panicked *late* feeling in Justin's stomach gave way to a different kind of horror.

He stopped cold.

Michael, whose right pinky was reaching for the very last pebble lodged deep in his right nostril, ran right into Justin, hitting his elbow against Justin's back and forcing the pebble even deeper up his nose. "*UGH!*" He grunted with the impact, which forced him to swallow the pebble.

"Oh. Thanks!" he said.

"We're lost," Justin whispered.

"We're *what*?" Michael asked.

"We're lost. I don't know where we are. I must have missed the turn!"

"That's not good," Michael said casually.

The boys looked at each other.
"AHHHHH!" they screamed in unison.

Being lost in a cave, whether it's in the Middle East or the middle of Tennessee, is most certainly not good.

"Fortunately," they would tell their friends when they were back at school later that year, "we had two years of Junior Ranger Patrol training!"

In reality, Michael just happened to remember the story of Hansel and Gretel.

"Why don't we just follow our footsteps back to where we're supposed to turn?" Michael said. "Like bread-crumbs."

"Oh. Yeah. Good idea," Justin said, looking slightly calmer.

Thirty minutes later, and one hour late for dinner, the boys spotted daylight.

CHAPTER 3

"Michael!!!"

Whenever Michael heard his name yelled, he knew he was in trouble. And he heard his name yelled a lot. According to his little sister, Jane, *Michael* was the most used word in the English language. But this time

Michael didn't mind hearing it. Being in trouble was nothing compared to being lost in a cave.

"Dad!" Michael ran to hug his father. "I am so happy to see you!"

"What were you doing?! What were you thinking!?! Why were you—?" Michael's dad stammered. "You can't just wander into a strange cave by yourself!"

"We were exploring!" Michael said pathetically. "Besides, Justin was with me . . ."

"It's also a strange cave for Justin!" his dad yelled.

"I know, I know. I'm sorry," Michael said.

"I'm sorry too, Dr. Gomez," said Justin.

"If I lost you two on our next-to-last

day here, I would be in big trouble with your mothers. Both of you are grounded until we ship out in the morning. Go to your tent!" Michael's dad ordered.

Usually when kids are grounded, they are sent to their rooms (in a house), so this may require further explanation. You see, Michael's dad was a college professor studying people who had lived in the Middle East thousands of years ago. He was working in an area close to where many of the stories from the Bible took place—from Joshua leading the Israelites into the Promised Land to David hiding from King Saul; from Elijah going up into heaven in a chariot of fire to John baptizing Jesus. Dr. Gomez thought coming along on the trip would be a good learning experience for his son. Michael, who was always up for an adventure, liked the idea, but he wasn't crazy about spending an entire summer away from his best friend, so he convinced his dad to invite Justin, too. For two months Michael and Justin shared a tent in the desert beside the Dead Sea in Israel. If you're wondering why it's named the Dead Sea, the answer is very simple: the water is so salty, fish can't survive in it. Have you

ever tasted ocean water? The Dead Sea is ten times saltier! Not only that, but the Dead Sea is smack-dab in the middle of a desert, so the land around it is hot, dry, and dusty. Very few plants or animals can survive in the harsh environment. But the land is still beautiful and, most importantly, fun for a couple of 10-year-olds. When they weren't busy helping to lug broken pieces of old pottery around, they spent their time capturing scorpions in pickle

jars, rolling down sand dunes, and, of course, exploring.

"Michael, I've told you before to never go into a cave without an experienced guide." Dr. Gomez leaned down and got eye to eye with his son. "I love that you love to explore, but it's important that you listen to me. It's for your own good, because I want what's best for you. Understand?"

"I understand," Michael said as they returned to camp.

CHAPTER 4

"Grounded on our last night here!" Michael whined as he lay on his cot, sketching.

"Well, we wouldn't be if you would've listened to your dad in the first place," Justin replied. "It's been a fun summer, though. Hard to believe we'll be back in a boring old classroom in a couple days."

"Yup." Michael sketched quietly for a moment, then asked, "Hey, when we entered the cave, did we take two rights and a left, or three rights?"

"Three rights, I think," Justin replied. "Um, what are you doing?"

"Drawing a map."

Justin knew Michael well enough to know that this could not be good.

"Michael, you are not going back into that cave."

Michael showed Justin his map. "Check it out! Here's the ledge. Don't you want to know what was up there? It could be a treasure. What if we made THE discovery of the summer? Wouldn't that be amazing?"

"WE? Don't bring ME into this!

And YOU are not going back into that cave." Justin crossed his arms. "Remember what your dad said? 'Never go into a cave without an experienced guide.' Those were his exact words."

"Exactly! I've been into that cave, and now I have a map of it. If that's not experience, I don't know what is!" Michael reasoned.

"Do us both a favor and forget about whatever is up on that ledge," Justin said.

"I'm not sure I can," Michael replied. "We leave tomorrow, and we may never come back. What if I go my whole life wondering what was up there?"

"I think the real question is, are you going to listen to your dad or not?" Justin said. He blew out the lantern between their cots and rolled over. "Good night."

"Good night," Michael replied, but his mind was racing, and he was not feeling the least bit sleepy. *So many questions,* he thought.

CHAPTER 5

When a boy's sense of curiosity outweighs his common sense, he can sometimes find himself alone in a cave in the Middle East in the middle of the night. It doesn't happen that often, but when it does, it usually means trouble. As hard as Michael tried to fall asleep, and as much as his conscience told him to stay in bed, in the end, he decided that he just had to know what was on that ledge.

I'm the son of a scientist, he reasoned to himself as he plodded through the cave with only the sound of his foot-steps on the dusty stone floor to keep him company. *Discovery is in my blood!* These thoughts helped him feel a little better. Conveniently, they also let him blame his dad for his decision not to listen to his dad.

The loud squeal of a bat pierced the silence.

AHHHHH!

The louder scream of a frightened boy followed.

Michael dropped both his flashlight and his map. He heard the creature's wings flapping behind him toward the mouth of the cave as he leaned against the rock wall, breathing heavily. The fact that a dead bat is what Michael was expecting to find at the end of his quest didn't do much to lessen his surprise. "It's just a bat. Bats live in caves," Michael said out loud, reassuring himself. He picked his flashlight back up, located the map, and was soon on his way again.

It turns out that Michael's memory—and his map-drawing skills—were pretty good. After about 20 minutes, three right turns, two left turns, and one more squealing bat encounter, Michael found himself exactly where he hoped to be—at the foot of the ledge.

Justin will be amazed when he sees what I bring back, Michael thought proudly as he took a length of rope out of his backpack. Holding tightly to one end, he tossed the other end of the rope up and over a rock that jutted out from the ledge. It looped smoothly over its target and fell softly at his feet. "This is almost too easy!" Michael said out loud, impressed with his own rope skills. "Yep. Exploring is definitely in my blood." He anchored one end of the rope to a heavy rock on the floor of the cave, put the flashlight in his mouth, and began his climb. In no time, he found himself peeking over the top of the ledge, his eyes going wide as he made his

discovery. If he hadn't had a flashlight in his mouth, he would have
said, "Whoa . . ." But since he did
have a flashlight in his mouth,
what came out was,

CHAPTER 6

"You guys up?" Michael's dad called from outside the tent.

Justin cracked open his eyes to see the dim light of daybreak. "Ummhmm," he managed to groan out in response.

"Okay. Let's get packed up. We've got a long day," Dr. Gomez said.

"C'mon, Michael. You heard him." Justin flopped an arm onto Michael's cot. His hand landed with a thud on an empty sleeping bag. Justin shot up, suddenly 100 percent awake. "Oh no!" he shouted out without thinking.

"Everything all right?" Dr. Gomez called.

Justin started to panic. He needed to buy some time to think. "Uh, yeah . . . everything's fine," he called. *Maybe Michael got up to go to the bathroom,* Justin thought. *No. His dad would have seen him.* Justin's eyes shot around the tent. Michael's boots, back-pack, flashlight—all gone. *He must have snuck away to the cave during the night.* The fact that he wasn't back yet could not be good. *Maybe he hasn't been gone for long and will be here any minute.* Justin sat back down with a thud on his cot. He knew better. Michael slept like a rock. He had to have left before he fell asleep, which meant he had been gone all night.

"Boys?" Dr. Gomez called out again. "Up and at 'em!"

Now Justin had a decision to make. Should he cover for his buddy? *If Michael went back into that cave, his dad will be furious!* he thought. Or should he sound the alarm? *If he's lost in that cave, his dad being upset will be the least of his worries.* Justin knew what he had to do.

The zipper on the tent door slid down, and Justin popped his head out. "Um . . . Dr. Gomez?"

CHAPTER 7

Michael's plan was going so well. His map had led him to exactly what he had gone looking for.

"Eww, gross!" Michael said as he hung from the rope with one hand. He held his flashlight in the other hand, illuminating a couple of dried-out and long-gone mammals, each about the size of a loaf of bread. (For Michael, like for a lot of 10-year-olds, "gross" meant pretty much the same thing as "cool.")

There was no way he wouldn't be taking these treasures back home with him. He placed the flashlight in his teeth to free up a hand then reached around and unzipped the top of his backpack. No sooner had he stashed the treasure in his pack than another bat came flapping past his face in the darkness.

Michael screamed.

The thing about "AHHHHH!" is that your mouth has to be all the way open to say it. And the thing about having your mouth all the way open is that anything you are holding with your teeth will fall out.

The flashlight hit the rocky cave floor, shattering the bulb and plunging Michael into complete darkness. If Michael had been a truly experienced cave explorer, he would have known to bring an extra flashlight, but he was not, and he did not.

"Uh-oh," Michael said, clinging to his rope. If anything is scarier than a random bat flying at your face, it's being suspended eight feet in the air in total darkness. Michael's first reaction was to reach for the ledge he remembered last seeing in front of him. Bad idea.

THUD! Michael hit the floor.

"Owwwww," he groaned. As much as falling hurt, at least he'd gotten it over with. His only other option had been to get stuck up on the ledge.

Michael felt around for his backpack, which had landed a few
feet over. *I need to get out of here!*
His map was still in his backpack.
A map that you can't see isn't at
all useful, but at least Michael
had drawn it. He reasoned his
best chance would be to retrace
his steps from memory. He
knew how many turns to take,
but could he remember *when* to
take them? Or would he just get
more lost in the cave? Maybe he

should stay put and count on Justin figuring out where he went and leading a rescue team to him? On the other hand, if he found his way out on his own, no one—especially his dad—would ever know he'd been gone.

Michael made his decision. "I gotta get back," he said out loud, the words bouncing off the cave walls. He wobbled to his feet, slung on his backpack, and stumbled forward into the darkness.

CHAPTER 8

Dr. Gomez, followed by Justin and a handful of workers, ran toward the mouth of the cave.

"How long has he been gone?" Michael's dad shouted over his shoulder to Justin.

"I don't know!" Justin answered. "Probably all night."

"Break up into three groups," Dr. Gomez ordered. "Justin, you come with me. Think you can remember where you were?"

"I think so."

Three groups of searchers, led by experienced cave guides with plenty of flash-lights, entered the cave.

"Yell if you find him!" Dr. Gomez shouted as the groups split up and headed into separate corridors in search of Michael.

CHAPTER 9

Michael walked sideways with his hands stretched out in front of him, feeling his way along the rocky cave wall in the darkness. He had no idea what time it was, but he felt like he had been lost for hours. He'd taken what he'd thought were all the correct turns, but here he still was, lost in the dark with no way of knowing if he was moving toward or away from the exit.

Maybe I should take a nap, he thought. He had been up all night, and he was exhausted. The thought of a giant cave spider or boy-eating mole discovering him in his sleep, however, was enough to keep his eyes open and his feet moving.

"Why didn't I listen to my dad?" Michael said out loud, his voice echoing through the corridors of the cave. "I wouldn't be in this mess if I had. I don't even care anymore if I get in trouble. Dad can ground me for a year—I just want to go home." Suddenly, he heard a noise coming from the distance. It sounded like legs scurrying along. Lots of legs. He froze, terrified, his heart pounding so hard he could feel it in his ears. What if it was the giant cave spider? (It sounded like it had too many legs to be a boy-eating mole.)

A narrow beam of light appeared on the wall about 50 feet in front of Michael. Because he'd been in total darkness for hours, just that little bit of light hurt his eyes, but it could only mean one thing.

"Thank you, God!" he prayed. "I'm here! I'm here!" he shouted.

Two men rounded the corner, carrying flashlights. Light flooded the cave corridor as they approached the tired, dirty, and squinting boy.

CHAPTER 10

"Michael!" Dr. Gomez shouted as he emerged from the cave with Justin. They ran over to where Michael was sitting with the men who had rescued him. Dr. Gomez hugged his son tightly. "Thank goodness you're all right! You had me worried sick."

"I'm so sorry, Dad," Michael said. "I should have listened to you."

Dr. Gomez took Michael's face in his hands and looked him straight in the eyes. "We're going to need to talk about this," he said sternly.

"Yes, sir."

Beep! Beep! A small car drove up the rocky path outside the caves, its rooftop packed with luggage and crates. The driver leaned out the window and called, "Dr. Gomez! Are we going?"

"If we hurry, we can still make our flight. C'mon, boys!"

Dr. Gomez jumped into the

front seat of the car while Michael and Justin piled into the back, and they sped off to the airport in a cloud of dust.

After a loud and extremely bumpy ride to reach the main road, Michael noticed a glare coming from the seat next to him. He turned his head slowly toward Justin and smiled sheepishly. "Sorry . . ."

"You should be!" Justin barked in a loud whisper, hoping to keep their conversation confined to the back seat. "I hope you're happy. What could have been so important that you had to go back into that cave to get it? You do realize you're going to be grounded for a year, right?"

Michael wiggled out of his backpack and unzipped the top, making sure to not draw any attention from the front seat, where his dad was busy talking to the driver about the fastest route to the airport.

"Check this out!" He reached inside the backpack and pulled out what appeared to be a bone-dry squirrel covered in a thick layer of salt.

"Ewww! What is that?" Justin got as far away from the object as he could.

"I think it's a squirrel," Michael replied. "Look, I've got another one."

He pulled another dried rodent out of his bag.

"Ewww!" Justin said again. "You have two? That's double gross! Get rid of those things. Who knows what kind of nasty disease we could catch?"

"No way." Michael patted the squirrels. "I'm bringing them home as souvenirs. Mementos of our awesome summer!"

"You can't do that!" Justin said.

"Why not?"

"It's probably not even legal—smuggling squirrels across international borders."

"It's not like taking a live plant or an artifact," Michael argued. "It's just a couple of petrified squirrels. Plus, they're so dry and salty, no germs could live on them."

Justin shook his head disapprovingly as Michael stuffed the stiff rodents back into his backpack.

CHAPTER 11

The car came to a screeching halt outside the airport. "Let's go, boys!" Dr. Gomez said, jumping out of the car. "Everybody grab a suitcase!" Michael and Justin grabbed as many bags as they could handle and headed inside.

"Get rid of those squirrels," Justin urged Michael. "There's no way they'll let them on the plane."

"I bring seashells back from vacation all the time," Michael responded. "It's the same thing."

"It is NOT the same thing!"

With only minutes remaining until their plane departed, Dr. Gomez and the boys rushed to the check-in counter and then to the security line. "I don't know if we're going to make it!" Michael's dad said nervously. "Quick, boys—backpacks on the X-ray belt!"

When Michael heard the word *X-ray* his heart sank. He had totally forgotten about the X-ray machine! His squirrels were sure to be discovered. "Um, Justin," he whispered, "I think you were right. Salty squirrels are not the same thing as seashells."

"You are so busted," Justin replied. "Grounded for two years, for sure."

"Whose is this?" a security officer demanded as he held up a backpack. Michael couldn't bear to look. He braced himself for what was coming.

"That's mine, sir," Michael heard his dad say. Confused, Michael looked up to see the officer holding a bottle of water.

A backpack showing the faint outline of two squirrel skeletons passed through the X-ray machine unnoticed.

"You have to get rid of this," the officer told Dr. Gomez, shaking the water bottle.

"Of course. Sorry," Michael's dad said. The officer threw the water bottle in the trash.

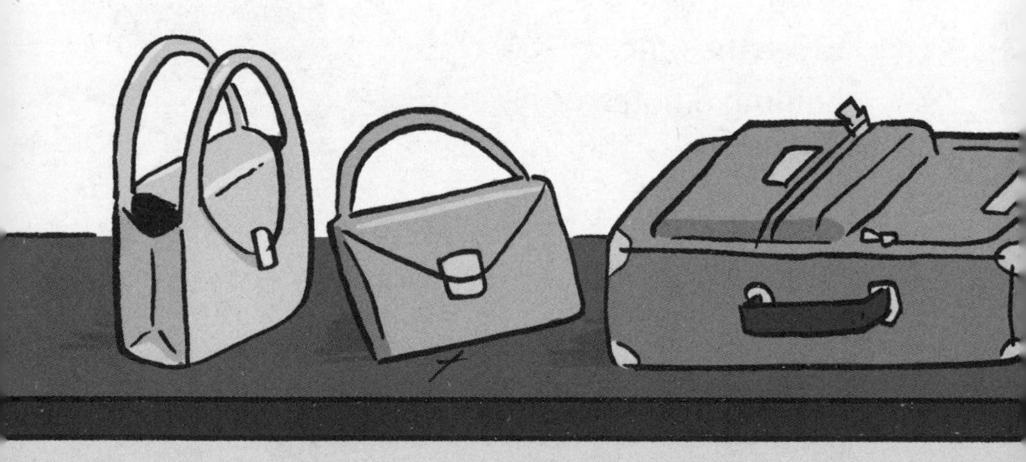

Michael grabbed his backpack the second it exited the machine. "Whew!" he gasped.

Justin shook his head in disbelief as they headed toward the gate.

CHAPTER 12

"Let me take that for you, sweetie," the flight attendant offered.

"No, it's okay—I got it!" Michael grunted as he kicked his backpack, trying to wedge it under the seat in front of him. He would feel a lot better if he could keep an eye on it himself during the flight.

"I don't think it's gonna fit, buddy," Dr. Gomez said from across the aisle.

"Yeah, Michael. You have too much stuff jammed in there," Justin said. He settled into the seat beside Michael and buckled in.

Michael looked back up at the smiling attendant.

"Can I keep it on my lap?" he asked.

"Sorry," she said, looking at him suspiciously and holding out her hand for the bag.

Michael reluctantly handed over his backpack, along with its questionable contents. The flight attendant placed it in an overhead bin a few seats up. "Have a nice flight," she said.

Surprisingly, with his bag locked snugly away, Michael felt like he could finally relax. And feeling like you can relax after you've been up all night fearing for your life in a pitch-black cave could only mean—

"Zzzzzzzzz." Michael was out cold, drooling on his tiny flight pillow.

CHAPTER 13

BOOM! Chukka chukka chukka . . .

Michael opened his eyes with a start. *How long have I been asleep?* He lifted his head from his drool-soaked pillow and looked around. It was daylight outside, but many of the passengers around him were sleeping.

DING! The red Fasten Seat Belt light flashed on above him.

"No big deal." Justin yawned. "Just a little rough air. Might as well go back to sleep."

Michael was happy to take the advice. He still felt exhausted. But before he could close his eyes again, he noticed that the overhead bin

where his backpack had been placed had been flung open by the turbulence.

"Oh no!" Michael gasped.

"What?" asked Justin.

Michael pointed at his backpack. The top was unzipped, and a crusty, scraggly squirrel tail was sticking out. Then the plane hit another pocket of rough air—and the bag slipped out and fell onto the back of the seat below!

"Ahhhhh!" Michael whispered, fighting to hold back a scream.

"Ahhhhh!" repeated Justin in a slightly louder whisper.

A squirrel slid out of the bag and onto the head of a sleeping man!

"AHHHHH!" Michael screamed, not in a whisper.

"Shhhhh!" Justin urged. "You're gonna wake up your dad!"

Michael looked across the aisle at his sleeping father. "I gotta get that squirrel!" he whispered to Justin. Michael looked up and down the aisle, checking for flight attendants. All clear. He unbuckled his belt quietly, stood up, and tiptoed forward.

The salty rodent tail covered the nose and mouth of the sleeping man, rising and falling slowly with his breathing. *Yuck!* Michael thought. As cool as he thought the squirrels were, he would not like one on his face! As he reached forward to grab it, a voice called out, "Young man! You need to remain in your seat!"

It was the flight attendant who had stowed his backpack.

Without looking at her, Michael grabbed the squirrel off the sleeping man's face, stuffed it back in his backpack, crammed the bag back into the overhead bin, and slammed the bin shut. He looked over to see the flight attendant standing in the aisle near the front of the plane, motioning to a dark-haired man seated next to her.

The man turned to look at Michael. He was wearing a suit and sunglasses and looked very official. *Who wears a suit and sunglasses on a 12-hour flight?* Michael thought.

"Sorry!" he called out as he scrambled back to his seat.

"Everything all right?" Dr. Gomez said sleepily as Michael sat back down and buckled up.

"Yeah. Everything's fine," Michael said. He peeked around the front of his seat to see the flight attendant giving him the stink eye as the man in the suit and sunglasses looked on with a steely gaze.

CHAPTER 14

COOKIES!

The shout echoed through the concourse as Michael walked out with his dad and Justin. Michael covered his face with his hands. *Cookies* was his mom's super-embarrassing nickname for him, and hearing it yelled out loud in public was THE WORST. Michael's mom waved at him wildly. Next to her stood Jane, Michael's little sister, who seemed surprisingly happy to see him too. Justin's mom was also there. It was hugs all around as the women welcomed their men back home after a long summer.

"Let me get that for you!" Mrs. Gomez offered, reaching for Michael's backpack.

"No, I got it." Michael didn't want to let it out of his sight until he got home. "And please don't call me Cookies. I'm in fifth grade now. Well, almost."

"Did you bring me anything?" asked Jane, who was four years old and about to start preschool, taught by Mrs. Gomez. Michael assumed this was necessary because his parents couldn't convince any other teachers to take Jane.

"Of course, sweetheart!" Dr. Gomez responded.

"What about you, Michael? Did you bring me something?"

"Um . . ." Before he could answer, Michael caught a glimpse of someone familiar. The man in the suit and sunglasses from the plane was standing about 30 feet away by the escalators, looking up at Michael over his phone. When the man noticed that he had been noticed, he quickly looked down at his phone, turned around, and went down the escalator.

"Well, did you?" Jane asked again.

"Was I supposed to?" Michael responded, distracted.

"You all must be exhausted!" Mrs. Gomez said. "Let's get you home!"

"See you in school tomorrow, Michael!" Justin said as he headed toward the escalator with his mom.

CHAPTER 15

DEAD SEA
AD 70

How did two squirrels get stuck in a cave, anyway? There are three types of squirrels: tree squirrels, which live in trees; ground squirrels, which live underground; and cave squirrels, which don't exist. Had Michael known that the "cave squirrel" has never been a thing, he might have asked himself the same question. And the answer? Vacation, of course!

"You know what I love most about the Dead Sea, Pearl?" Merle said as he waded into the super salty water.

“What could you possibly love about this awful place?” Pearl responded from behind her little sunglasses, lying on her little lounge chair under her little beach umbrella. “It’s too hot, it’s too dry, and it’s waaaaay too salty.”

“That’s the best part! Woohoo!” Merle jumped high into the air and landed flat on his back on the surface of the water. *SPLASH!* “Oooof!” He

grunted with the force of the impact. "Look! You can't sink!"

"That's just great, Merle. We came all this way to see you not sink." Pearl wiped the salty splash out of her eyes. "Couldn't you have just worn your floaties in the lake back home?"

"It's not the same," Merle replied, using his tail to swirl around in circles on the water. "I've always wanted to

not sink!" Merle turned over and tried to dive down under the water, only to pop right back up. "Pffffft!" He spit out a mouthful of salty water. "Wow. That IS salty."

"Well, it is nice to get away," Pearl said, shifting her umbrella aside so she could bask in the sun. "And it was a relaxing raft ride down the Jordan."

"Made that raft myself!" Merle said proudly, returning to floating on his back.

"You've always been good with your paws," Pearl complimented him.

"Now I just have to figure out how we're gonna get back."

Pearl sat straight up in her tiny lounge chair. "What?!"

"Well, the river only carries a raft one way, and that's here."

Merle was a squirrel who loved to explore, and now that the pups were out of the tree and off on their own, he was itching to travel and see the world. Sometimes, however, Merle didn't think things all the way through.

Pearl sighed. "Merle, sometimes you just don't think things through."

CHAPTER 16

"I'm sooooo hooooot!" Merle groaned as he and Pearl huddled under the tiny bit of shade cast by the umbrella. He'd had his fill of not sinking and now was hoping for some relief from the sun.

"It doesn't help that we're both covered in fur and hugging," Pearl responded.

"We have to get out of this sun! Why aren't there any trees around here?" Merle complained.

"My guess is because it's the desert."

Merle spotted a rocky cliffside along the shoreline. "Let's head over there," he suggested. "Maybe we can find some better shade. Maybe even a cave!"

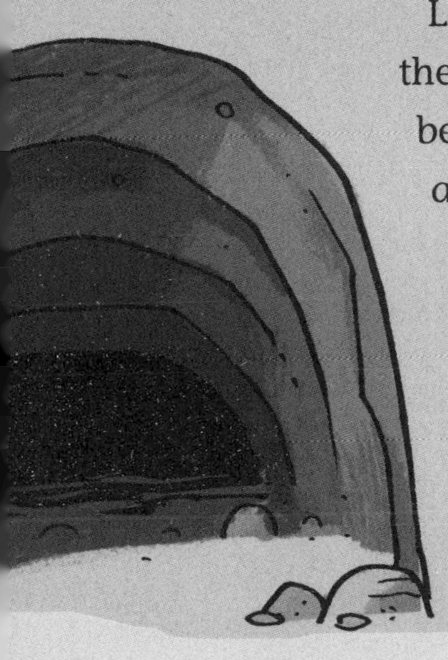

Leaving their raft behind, the two picked up their beach chair and umbrella and headed for the cliffs, their stiff, salt-covered fur crackling as they walked. Before long, they spotted an opening in the rocks with a large, beautiful pool of shade underneath. The squirrels ran toward it and collapsed on the cool, sandy ground.

Pearl, the more sensible of the two, suggested they wait in the shade until nightfall and then look for a town or a camel caravan.

"Good idea." Then Merle realized something. "Hey . . . I've never been in a cave!"

"Don't get any ideas," Pearl warned. "There are only two types of squirrels: tree squirrels and ground squirrels—"

"—and if God wanted you to mess around in caves, he would have made you a bat," Merle continued. "My dad always told me the same thing. 'Never go into a cave!' he said."

"That's great advice, Merle." Pearl tried to brush some of the salt off her fur. "Remember what Paul said? 'Honor your father and your mother.'"

"Moses said it first. Besides, I'm a full-grown squirrel!" Merle said.

"Actually, God said it first, and you're never too old for good advice." Pearl shook her finger at him.

"But it looks so interesting and cool—like temperature cool—back there, Pearl. Let's just go have a quick look." Without waiting for an answer, Merle crept further inside the mouth of the cave.

CHAPTER 17

WALNUT CREEK, TENNESSEE
PRESENT DAY

With the long day and long summer now behind him, Michael was glad to finally be back in his own room and his own bed. Like always, he prayed with his parents before bedtime.

"Thank you, God, for an awesome summer. Thank you for all the fun I had with Dad and Justin, thank you for keeping us safe, and thank you especially that I didn't stay lost in that cave. Amen."

WAIT... WHAT?!

his mom shouted. "Lost in a cave?"

"Yeah . . ." His dad said. "I've been meaning to talk with you about that. Michael, you want to tell your mom what happened?"

"Okay. Justin and I were exploring a cave and got a little bit lost, but eventually we found our way out. Dad told me to never do that again, but I didn't listen. I went back in later by myself and got a whole lot lost when my flashlight broke."

Mrs. Gomez went pale. "You were by yourself in a cave with no flashlight?"

"It's okay, Mom. I'm fine now."

"Michael, you know that when we ask you to do something or to not do something, it's for your own good, right?" Dr. Gomez said. "The Bible tells us that honoring your father and mother is the first commandment with a promise. When you do, things will go well for you and you will live longer."

"Yeah, I get the 'live longer' part now," Michael said.

"Look, buddy. We're older and have a lot more experience with life, which makes us a little wiser than you. We love you and want what's best for you." Dr. Gomez ruffled Michael's hair.

"Thanks, Dad," Michael said. "I love you guys, too."

"By the way, what was so important that you needed to go back into that cave for it?" Mrs. Gomez asked.

"*Meow!*" Mr. Nemesis, Jane's cat, said from across the room. He was scratching at Michael's backpack.

Michael jumped out of bed. "Get off that!" he yelled, chasing Mr. Nemesis out of the room.

"C'mon, back in bed," Dr. Gomez said. "We've all got school in the morning. No time for chasing cats around."

Michael crawled back into bed. His mom and dad kissed him on the head. Dr. Gomez turned off the light. Just before closing the door, he said, "By the way, you're grounded for a week."

"Dad!" Michael complained.

"Good night, Cookies!" Mrs. Gomez said.

"Don't call me that!" Michael double-complained.

CHAPTER 18

When you're excited because tomorrow is your first day of fifth grade—which, in case you didn't know, makes you elementary school royalty—and when you are not all that tired anyway because you slept pretty much the whole day on a plane, going to sleep is not easy. Michael lay awake thinking about his summer and about the year ahead. He couldn't wait to see his friends and tell them about his and Justin's adventures. Their friend Sadie, in particular, would love hearing all about it. At school, they were pretty much the Three Musketeers, and Michael had been bummed that Sadie couldn't join them in Israel.

Michael's thoughts turned to the squirrels in his backpack. He couldn't leave them in there forever. They were, after all, souvenirs. He would need to tell his parents about them sooner or later. Michael threw his covers off and took the crusty critters out of his backpack. He held them up, wondering if all the trouble he had gone through to get them to his house was worth it. *I hope they don't stink up my room,* he thought.

Looking around his room to find the best place to display his treasures, Michael decided on the top of his dresser. They would show up best from the highest point in the room. He propped the squirrels up, surprised to discover that, with some gentle pushing and pulling, he was able to arrange their arms and legs so that they could stand up, like posable action figures.

"Awesome," he whispered.

He'd made the squirrels look like fierce nut-hoarding warriors. "Sadie is going to think these are so cool." He thought for a moment about taking them to school the next day but decided it was too risky. Besides, he needed a break from the stress of toting them around. Being grounded meant that he would have to come straight home after class, but maybe Justin and Sadie could drop by for a quick look.

Michael opened the window next to his dresser to help with any possible odor issues. A cool late-summer breeze blew in, and the low rumble of distant thunder sounded as Michael crawled back into bed.

He closed his eyes and eventually drifted off to sleep as a light, misty rain sprinkled through the screen, dampening the top of the dresser—and the dry, salty fur of Michael's souvenir squirrels. If the rain had been heavier, Michael probably would have woken up. And if he'd woken up, he might have seen the paw of one of the squirrels move ever so slightly. But it was not, and he did not.

MICHAEL GOMEZ is an adventurous and active 10-year-old boy. He is kindhearted but often acts before he thinks. He's friendly and talkative and blissfully unaware that most of his classmates think he's a bit geeky. Michael is super excited to be in fifth grade, which, in his mind, makes him "grade school royalty!"

MERLE SQUIRREL may be thousands of years old, but he never really grew up. He has endless enthusiasm for anything new and interesting—especially this strange modern world he finds himself in. He marvels at the self-refilling bowl of fresh drinking water (otherwise known as a toilet) and supplements his regular diet of tree nuts with what he believes might be the world's most perfect food: chicken nuggets. He's old enough to know better, but he often finds it hard to do better. Good thing he's got his wife, Pearl, to help him make wise choices.

PEARL SQUIRREL is wise beyond her many, many, many years, with enough common sense for both her and Merle. When Michael's in a bind, she loves to share a lesson or bit of wisdom from Bible events she witnessed in her youth. Pearl's biggest quirk is that she is a nut hoarder. Having come from a world where food is scarce, her instinct is to grab whatever she can. The abundance and variety of nuts in present-day Tennessee can lead to distraction and storage issues.

JUSTIN KESSLER is Michael's best friend. Justin is quieter and has better judgment than Michael, and he is super smart. He's a rule follower and is obsessed with being on time. He'll usually give in to what Michael wants to do after warning him of the likely consequences.

SADIE HENDERSON is Michael and Justin's other best friend. She enjoys video games and bowling just as much as cheerleading and pajama parties. She gets mad respect from her classmates as the only kid at Walnut Creek Elementary who's not afraid of school bully Edgar. Though Sadie's in a different homeroom than her two best friends, the three always sit together at lunch and hang out after class.

CHARACTER PROFILE

DR. GOMEZ, a professor of anthropology, is not thrilled when he finds out that his son, Michael, smuggled two ancient squirrels home from their summer trip to the Dead Sea, but he ends up seeing great value in having them around as original sources for his research. Dad loves his son's adventurous spirit but wishes Michael would look (or at least peek) before he leaps.

MRS. GOMEZ teaches part-time at her daughter's preschool and is a full-time mom to Michael and Jane. She feels sorry for the fish-out-of-water squirrels and looks for ways to help them feel at home, including constructing and decorating an over-the-top hamster mansion for Merle and Pearl in Michael's room. She also can't help but call Michael by her favorite (and his least favorite) nickname, Cookies.

MR. NEMESIS is the Gomez family cat who becomes Merle and Pearl's true nemesis. Jealous of the time and attention given to the squirrels by his family, Mr. Nemesis is continuously coming up with brilliant and creative ways to get rid of them. He hides his ability to talk from the family, but not the squirrels.

JANE GOMEZ is Michael's little sister. She's super adorable but delights in getting her brother busted so she can be known as the "good child." She thinks Merle and Pearl are the cutest things she has ever seen in her whole life (next to Mr. Nemesis) and is fond of dressing them up in her doll clothes.

DR. GOMEZ'S
Historical Handbook

So now you've heard of the Dead Sea Squirrels, but what about the

DEAD SEA *SCROLLS*?

Way back in 1946, just after the end of World War II, in a cave along the banks of the Dead Sea, a 15-year-old boy came across some jars containing ancient scrolls while looking after his goats. When scholars and archaeologists found out about his discovery, the hunt for more scrolls was on! Over the next 10 years, many more scrolls and pieces of scrolls were found in 11 different caves.

There are different theories about exactly who wrote on the scrolls and hid them in the caves. One of the most popular ideas is that they belonged to a group of Jewish priests called Essenes, who lived in the desert because they had been thrown out of Jerusalem. One thing is for sure—the scrolls are very, very old! They were placed in the caves between the years 300 BC and AD 100 !

Forty percent of the words on the scrolls come from the Bible. Parts of every Old Testament book except for the book of Esther have been discovered.

Of the remaining 60 percent, half are religious texts not found in the Bible, and half are historical records about the way people lived 2,000 years ago.

The discovery of the Dead Sea Scrolls is one of the most important archaeological finds in history!

About the Author

As co-creator of VeggieTales, co-founder of Big Idea Entertainment, and the voice of the beloved Larry the Cucumber, **MIKE NAWROCKI** has been dedicated to helping parents pass on biblical values to their kids through storytelling for over two decades. Mike currently serves as Assistant Professor of Film and Animation at Lipscomb University in Nashville, Tennessee, and makes his home in nearby Franklin with his wife, Lisa, and their two children. The Dead Sea Squirrels is Mike's first children's book series.

DID THAT FOSSILIZED SQUIRREL JUST MOVE?

The Dead Sea Squirrels might not be as dead as Michael thought! How can he explain this one to his parents?

THE
DEAD SEA
SQUIRRELS
Boy Meets
Squirrels
From the co-creator of VeggieTales
Mike Nawrocki
Illustrated by Luke Séguin-Magee
Find out what happens when
Boy Meets Squirrels!

Watch out for more adventures with
Merle, Pearl, and all their friends!

CP1478

Join twelve-year-old Winnie Willis and her friends—both human and animal—on their adventures through paddock and pasture as they learn about caring for others, trusting God, and growing up.

Collect all eight Winnie the Horse Gentler books.
Or get the complete collection with the Barn Boxed Set!

CP1423